PEDRO FOR
PRESIDENT

by Fran Manushkin

illustrated by
Tammie Lyon

PICTURE WINDOW BOOKS
a capstone imprint

Pedro is published by Picture Window Books,
a Capstone Imprint
1710 Roe Crest Drive
North Mankato, Minnesota 56003
www.mycapstone.com

Text © 2017 Fran Manushkin
Illustrations © 2017 Picture Window Books

Library of Congress Cataloging-in-Publication Data

Names: Manushkin, Fran, author. | Lyon, Tammie, illustrator.
Title: Pedro for president / by Fran Manushkin ; [illustrated] by Tammie Lyon.
Description: North Mankato, Minnesota : Picture Window Books, a Capstone imprint, [2017] | Series: Pedro | Summary: Pedro runs for class president against his friend Katie Woo.
Identifiers: LCCN 2016002726| ISBN 9781515800873 (library binding) | ISBN 9781515800910 (pbk.) | ISBN 9781515800958 (ebook (pdf))
Subjects: LCSH: Woo, Katie (Fictitious character)—Juvenile fiction. | Elections—Juvenile fiction. | Speech—Juvenile fiction. | Hispanic Americans—Juvenile fiction. | Elementary schools—Juvenile fiction. | Friendship—Juvenile fiction. | CYAC: Hispanic Americans—Fiction. | Elections—Fiction. | Speech—Fiction. | Schools—Fiction. | Friendship—Fiction.
Classification: LCC PZ7.M3195 Pbg 2017 | DDC 813.54—dc23
LC record available at http://lccn.loc.gov/2016002726

Designers: Aruna Rangarajan and Tracy McCabe

Design Elements: Shutterstock

Photo Credits:
Greg Holch, pg. 26
Tammie Lyon, pg. 26

Printed and bound in the United States of America.
2205

Table of Contents

Chapter 1

Running for President

Pedro told Miss Winkle, "I am running for president of our class."

"So am I!" said Katie Woo.

Miss Winkle asked them,

"What can you do for our

class?"

"I can do

magic tricks,"

said Pedro.

"I can tap

dance," said Katie.

"Those are fun," said Miss
Winkle. "But how will you
help the class?"

"I don't know," said Katie.

"I'll have to think," said
Pedro.

That night, Pedro painted
a poster.

His brother Paco wanted to
help. He put his messy hands
all over it.

"I can fix this," said Pedro.

He painted:

VOTE FOR PEDRO!

I WILL GIVE YOU

A HELPING HAND!

"Good work," said his father.

"You are using your head."

Chapter 2
Speechless Pedro

The next day, Miss Winkle

said, "Before we vote tomorrow,

Katie and Pedro will each give

a speech. You can tell us why

you should be president."

"I'm not good at giving speeches," said Pedro.

"I am," bragged Katie Woo.

Pedro tried to write his speech. Just then, Roddy threw a pencil at the goldfish bowl. Pedro jumped up and caught the pencil.

"You saved our fish!"

cheered Barry. "And you

found my favorite pencil."

Pedro tried to write his speech again. But he saw JoJo looking sad.

"What's wrong?" he asked.

"I got a bad grade on my math test," said JoJo.

"Don't worry," said Pedro. "You can do better tomorrow. Maybe I can cheer you up with a joke."

Pedro asked, "Why is 6 afraid of 7?"

"Why?" asked JoJo.

"Because 7 8 9."

"That's funny," said JoJo. "I feel better."

That night, Pedro asked his dad, "What should I say in my speech tomorrow?"

"Arf!" barked Peppy.

"I can't say that!" Pedro joked.

Chapter 3

A Team-Player President

The next day was the

election. Katie gave a great

speech.

Miss Winkle asked Pedro,

"Is your speech ready?"

"Um, no," said Pedro.

Roddy yelled, "I want a boy to win. And I know what we should do."

"What?" asked JoJo.

Roddy said, "There are more boys than girls in this class. If all the boys vote for Pedro, he will win!"

"That's not fair!" said

Pedro. "You should vote for

the best person — boy or girl."

"That was a wonderful speech," said Miss Winkle.

"I'm voting for Pedro," said Barry.

"Me too!" said JoJo. "Pedro is a team player!"

Pedro asked Katie, "Will we still be friends if I win?"

"For sure!" said Katie. "We will always be friends."

They shook on it.

The class counted the votes.

Guess who won?

Pedro!

"I promise to be a terrific

president for everyone," he said.

And he was!

About the Author

Fran Manushkin is the author
of many popular picture books,
including *Happy in Our Skin*; *Baby,
Come Out!*; *Latkes and Applesauce:
A Hanukkah Story*; *The Tushy
Book*; *The Belly Book*; and *Big Girl
Panties*. Fran writes on her beloved
Mac computer in New York City, without the
help of her two naughty cats, Chaim and Goldy.

About the Illustrator

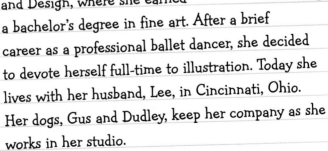

Tammie Lyon began her love for
drawing at a young age while
sitting at the kitchen table with
her dad. She continued her love
of art and eventually attended
the Columbus College of Art
and Design, where she earned
a bachelor's degree in fine art. After a brief
career as a professional ballet dancer, she decided
to devote herself full-time to illustration. Today she
lives with her husband, Lee, in Cincinnati, Ohio.
Her dogs, Gus and Dudley, keep her company as she
works in her studio.

Glossary

bragged (BRAGGED)—talked about how good you are at something

election (ih-LEK-shuhn)—the act of choosing someone to be a leader of a certain group

poster (POH-stur)—a large sign that often has a picture

president (PREZ-uh-duhnt)—the head of a company, club, or class

speech (SPEECH)—a talk given to a group of people

terrific (tuh-RIF-ik)—very good or excellent

vote (VOHT)—to make a choice in an election

Let's Talk

1. What are some of the things that Pedro did to help his classmates in the story?

2. The class president is a leader in the classroom. What makes a good leader? Use examples from the story and also think of your own.

3. How do you think Katie felt when she heard Roddy's idea? How do you think she felt when she heard Pedro's response?